Sights I Love to See

By Cheryl Willis Hudson • Illustrated by Laura Freeman

MARIMBA BOOKS

An imprint of The Hudson Publishing Group LLC.

Text copyright © 2017 by Cheryl Willis Hudson. Illustrations copyright © 2017 by Laura Freeman.

All Marimba Books titles are available at special quantity discounts for bulk purchases including sales promotions, premiums, fundraising and educational or instructional use. Specific book excerpts or customized printings can also be created for to meet specific needs.

For details contact the publisher. MARIMBA BOOKS, P.O. Box 5306, East Orange, NJ 07019, 973.672.7701   JustUsBooks.com

MARIMBA BOOKS and the Marimba Books logo are trademarks of The Hudson Publishing Group LLC.

ISBN-13: 978-1-60349-009-2

10 9 8 7 6 5 4 3 2 1

Printed in the United States of America

MARIMBA
BOOKS

There are wonderful sights I love to see.

They're all so familiar, yet special to me.

A glistening rainbow in the sky.
Billowing clouds passing by.

An army of ants on the move.

A blade of grass in a sandy groove.

Dew drops on the windowsill.
A chipmunk standing perfectly still.

Milkweed floating in the breeze.
Colors changing in the leaves.

A squiggling earthworm after a shower.

The pretty blooms of a springtime flower.

Snowflakes melting one by one.
Shadows changing under the sun.

Frothy waves by the ocean side.

My baby brother trying to hide.

Reflections in a silver spoon.

The man who's winking in the moon.

Fuzzy stripes on a bumblebee.

Candles on a cake just for me.

Jelly beans from the corner store.

Patterns on the kitchen floor.

Toes under water when I sit in the tub.

Bubbles that float when I rub-a-dub dub.

There are lots of sights I love to see.
But the best is *my* family smiling back at me.

CPSIA information can be obtained
at www.ICGtesting.com
Printed in the USA
BVOW05s1439150517
483671BV00001B/1/P